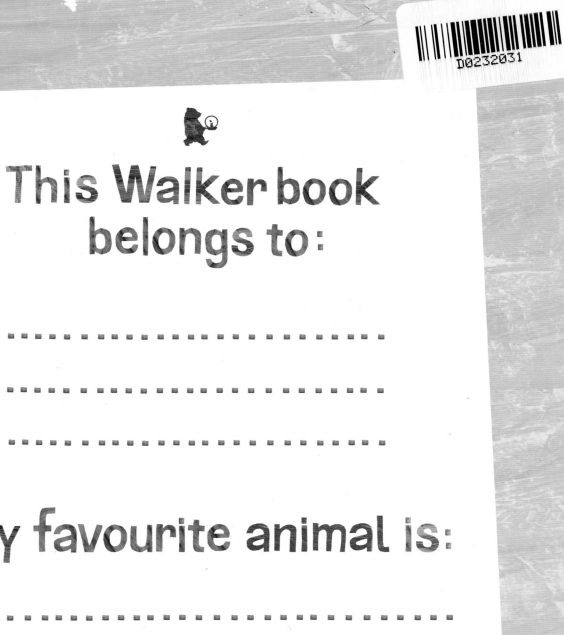

This Walker book belongs to:

....

....

....

My favourite animal is:

....

915 00000085045

D0232031

LEWISHAM LIBRARY SERVICE	
Askews & Holts	13-Mar-2015
J590 JUNIOR NON-FICT	1 J

First published in Great Britain 2014 by Walker Books Ltd
87 Vauxhall Walk, London SE11 5HJ

This edition published 2015

2 4 6 8 10 9 7 5 3 1

Compilation copyright © 2014 Eric Carle

First published in the United States 2014 by Henry Holt.
Published by arrangement with Henry Holt and Company LLC.

Permission to reproduce the following is gratefully acknowledged:
"Cats" © 2014 by Eric Carle; "Giraffe" © 2014 by Tom Lichtenheld; "Tink-Tink" © 2014 by Mo Willems;
"Blue Carp" © 2014 by Peter Sís; "The Snail" © 2014 by Chris Raschka; "Behold the Octopus" © 2014 by Nick Bruel;
"Bunnies" © 2014 by Peter McCarty; "A Dog on My Bed" © 2014 by Rosemary Wells;
"Elephant" © 2014 by Lane Smith; "Penguins" © 2014 by Erin Stead; "Leopard" © 2014 by Lucy Cousins.

The right of Eric Carle and his friends, Nick Bruel, Lucy Cousins, Susan Jeffers, Steven Kellogg,
Jon Klassen, Tom Lichtenheld, Peter McCarty, Chris Raschka, Peter Sís, Lane Smith, Erin Stead,
Rosemary Wells and Mo Willems to be identified as authors and illustrators of this work has
been asserted by them in accordance with the Copyright, Designs and Patents Act 1988

Printed in China

All rights reserved. No part of this book may be reproduced, transmitted or stored in
an information retrieval system in any form or by any means, graphic, electronic, or mechanical,
including photocopying, taping and recording, without prior written permission from the publisher.

British Library Cataloguing in Publication Data:
a catalogue record for this book is available from the British Library.

ISBN 978-1-4063-6000-4

Visit www.walker.co.uk
and www.carlemuseum.org

Eric Carle and Friends

What's Your Favourite Animal?

Nick Bruel • Lucy Cousins • Susan Jeffers

Steven Kellogg • Jon Klassen • Tom Lichtenheld

Peter McCarty • Chris Raschka • Peter Sís

Lane Smith • Erin Stead

Rosemary Wells • Mo Willems

WALKER BOOKS
AND SUBSIDIARIES
LONDON • BOSTON • SYDNEY • AUCKLAND

CATS
ERIC CARLE

I have always liked all animals. But CATS are my favourites. I have a photograph of myself when I was three years old, holding a couple of kittens. And I am sneezing. I must have been allergic to them, but my mother claimed I had a cold.

Later when I was grown up, Fiffi lived with me in my Greenwich Village New York City walk-up. Fiffi was a long-haired black beauty. One day when I was peeling string beans in the kitchen, she showed great interest in my task. After a while she even began to meow ever so slightly. It sounded like begging to me. Finally I threw a string bean down the long hallway. Fiffi chased after it, fetched it, and returned it to me. Again I threw the string bean down the hallway. Finally, after many chases, Fiffi picked up the string bean, ignored me and walked into the closet. She placed it into a shoe of mine. Then she curled herself around the shoe and went to sleep, guarding the string bean.

GIRAFFES
TOM LICHTENHELD

Though meeting a giraffe is rare,
You must be prepared not to stare.
They're easily amused,
So don't be confused.
Just say, "Hey, how's the weather up there?"

My favourite animal is an Amazonian Neotropical Lower River Tink-Tink.

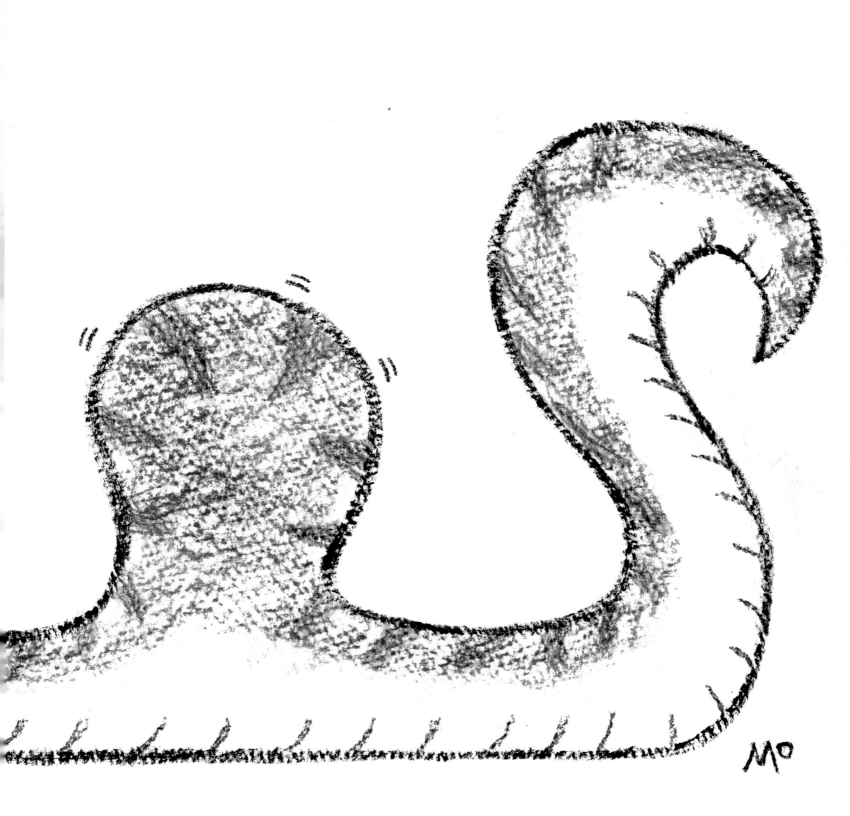

(It is also this snake's favourite animal.)

BLUE CARP
PETER SÍS

I am from the Czech Republic where people eat carp every Christmas Eve. It is a tradition. Just before the Christmas holidays, giant barrels with live carp are set up in the streets so people can buy one and bring it home fresh. There, they let the carp swim in the bathtub until

Christmas Eve. The carp would look all blue and lonely in the bathtub, and we, the children, would be fascinated and give her a name and try to put our little fingers in her toothless, breathing mouth. What usually happened on Christmas Eve when the carp is supposed to become a dinner was that the children would cry, go on strike, and finally the carp would be taken by the whole family to the river Vltava and released. You would see many families coming with their carps to the river and blue fish swimming toward the ocean. This gave us all hope! So my favourite creature of hope is the blue carp.

BEHOLD THE OCTOPUS

Octopuses are amazing. The more I learn about them, the more I admire them.

GIANT PACIFIC OCTOPUS

For instance, they are masters of camouflage. They have these things called chromatophores in their skin that can not only change their colour when they want to hide, but can change their texture, too.

MIMIC OCTOPUS HIDING IN/AS SAND

When they need to escape, they can squirt ink into the water to create a distraction and get away.

COMMON OCTOPUS

Octopuses have three hearts. THREE! Two hearts to pump blood to... Excuse me, Kitty, I'm working here ... their lungs, and the third to pump blood everywhere else.

BLUE-RINGED OCTOPUS

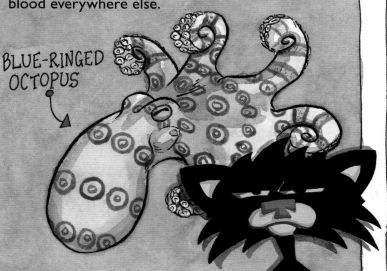

And boy are they smart! Kitty! Please! You're in the way! Octopuses are hard to keep as pets because they're so good at escaping any tank.

ATLANTIC WHITE-SPOTTED OCTOPUS

OK, Kitty.
What's the problem?

I see. You're jealous. Is it because I chose an octopus instead of a cat as my favourite animal?

No? Hmmm. Oh, now I get it! You're angry because I was asked and not YOU.

OK then, Kitty. What's YOUR favourite animal?

MEATLOAF? Meatloaf is not an animal. Try again.

ERIC CARLE?! Your favourite animal is Eric Carle?

Eric Carle is not an animal. (Well, arguably I guess he is.) But, Kitty, this shameless flattery is just not...

Wait. Did ... did Eric Carle just send you a present? What is it?

A MEATLOAF?! Eric Carle just sent you a meatloaf? Hmmm... This gives me an idea...

GOBBLE! SLURP! GULP!

Dear Eric Carle,
You are my most favouritest author! Sincerely,
NICK BRUEL

PS Please send me an Octopus.

BUNNIES
Peter McCarty

We have a bunny. I can't believe this bunny. He eats out of his favourite ceramic bowl, drinks from a water dispenser and poops and pees in a litter box!

I thought we might get a guinea pig. But this guy is no guinea pig. When he is happy he jumps straight up into the air and kicks his feet. His name is Mr Hopper, and he is a real member of our family. He even chases after the dog and cat when he wants to play.

A Dog on My Bed
ROSEMARY WELLS

A dog on my bed,
Right next to my head,
A little bit fuzzy, a little bit fat,
Nothing is more important than that!

Position 1

Position 2

Position 3

Position 4

Position 5

ELEPHANT
LANE SMITH

I was trying to decide what my favourite animal was when an elephant reminded me that pachyderms were my favourite.

I asked, "What's a pachyderm?"

The elephant said, "It's an elephant."

I said, "Why didn't you just say elephant?"

Elephants are my favourite animals.

But sometimes they are show-offs.

DUCK

Jon Klassen

Most times when you
see a duck in a story,
it's not very smart.
Usually it is in the
middle of falling
for a trick somebody
is playing on it.
But I like ducks.
I like watching them
walk around.

HORSES
Susan Jeffers

My sister and I shared a room when we were little, and we have shared a lifelong love of horses.

In the summer, our parents would put us to bed while it was still light out. After having a child of my own I understand why now. We would talk each other to sleep. One of our favourite topics was what colour horse we would choose if we could have any horse in our fantasy pasture. Judy loved palominos, golden coloured with a white mane and tail.

I could never decide between the deepest black or the purest white.

I usually went with pure white...

COWS
Steven Kellogg

As a boy, dreaming of becoming an artist, I drew and painted animals constantly and I wallpapered my room with the pictures. My older sister had claimed horses as her favourite animal, so I chose cows. I suspected that the cows in my drawings came to life during the night, because there was a place at the top of my head where the hair stood up that my grandmother said was a "cowlick."

After a few years had passed, and I could ride my bike far beyond our neighbourhood, I looked for jobs taking care of animals. No one had cows, but I was very happy when the owners of some beautiful English setters asked me to work in their kennel.

PENGUINS
Erin Stead

I have been known to say that I like animals more than people. It's not really true. I love people, but sometimes being around them makes me feel shy and nervous. I never feel uncomfortable around animals though.

An animal I really like to be around and watch is the penguin. If I visit a zoo, I can't wait to spend some time at the penguinarium. There are so many different types of personalities to see. I like how penguins seem confidently awkward on land but then glide so swiftly and expertly underwater. I think I relate to that a little.

I love leopards because
yellow is my favourite colour,
and their spots are SO beautiful.

Eric Carle has loved animals since he was a child, especially cats. He is the author and illustrator of more than 70 books, including *The Very Hungry Caterpillar* and *Brown Bear, Brown Bear, What Do You See?* written by Bill Martin Jr. Eric was born in the United States, but spent his early years in Stuttgart, Germany, where he studied art and design at the Academy of Applied Art. [eric-carle.com]

Tom Lichtenheld is a children's book author and illustrator. He doodled his way through school then worked as a sign painter, set designer, printer and advertising art director. After a successful career in advertising, he gradually made the switch to creating children's books. Tom's books are consistently praised for their humour, expressive characters, and rich – sometimes hidden – detail. He's known for creating books that appeal to children and adults alike, and his wide portfolio of books offers something for every age. In his spare time Tom enjoys chocolate, riding his bike, and getting other peoples' kids all wound up, then sending them home. [tomlichtenheld.com]

Mo Willems' work in children's books, animation, television, theatre, and bubble gum card paintings have garnered him three Caldecott Honors, two Geisel Medals, six Emmy Awards, three Geisel Honors, a Helen Hayes nomination and multiple bubble gum cards. Best known for his characters: Knuffle Bunny, The Pigeon and Elephant and Piggie, Mo's drawings, ceramics and sculptures have been exhibited in museums across the nation, including The Eric Carle Museum of Picture Book Art. He is still no good at cat hugging. [mowillems.com]

Peter Sís, recipient of a 2003 MacArthur Fellowship, was born in Brno, Moravia, and now lives in New York. He has created 26 award-winning animated shorts and films, stage designs, and murals, and has written and illustrated over 60 books for adults and children, including three Caldecott Honor books: *Starry Messenger*, *Tibet Through the Red Box* and *The Wall*. He received the Hans Christian Andersen award for his body of work in 2012. [petersis.com]

Chris Raschka is a two-time winner of the Caldecott Medal, and rarely comes out of his shell. When he does, he likes to paint dogs (*A Ball for Daisy*), birds (*Charlie Parker Played Be Bop*), hippos (*The Blushful Hippopotamus*), fish (*Arlene Sardine*), and sometimes even children (*Everyone Can Learn to Ride a Bicycle*). He lives with his family in New York City, where his favourite chair is almost always occupied by a cat.

Nick Bruel is the author and illustrator of the popular Bad Kitty series, which appears both in the picture book and chapter book formats, as well as the books *Bob and Otto*, *Who Is Melvin Bubble?* and *A Wonderful Year*. He lives in Tarrytown, New York, with his wife, Carina, their daughter, Izzy, and their noisy, hungry, cat, Esmerelda. [nickbruel.com]

Peter McCarty spent most of his childhood in his head. To this day, he develops characters and environments based on worlds he first created when he was three. *Little Bunny on the Move*, a *New York Times* Best Illustrated Book of the Year, came to him after months of searching for a story and established his career as an author–illustrator. Peter remains particularly fond of bunnies. [petermccarty.net]

Rosemary Wells, a bestselling author and illustrator of children's books throughout the world, has been drawing ever since she can remember. Her many books include *Max's Dragon Shirt*, *Max & Ruby's Bedtime Book*, and many other stories about Max and Ruby. She has recently published *Time-Out for Sophie* and *Sophie's Terrible Twos*, which are about a naughty two-year-old mouse named Sophie, and her wise and canny grandmother. Rosemary is passionate about animals of all kinds, especially West Highland terriers. Her own Westie is called Sophie, too. [rosemarywells.com]

Lane Smith was named a Carle Honor Artist in 2012. He is a four-time recipient of the *New York Times* Best Illustrated Book Award and a two-time Caldecott Honor recipient for *The Stinky Cheese Man* in 1993 and *Grandpa Green* in 2012. In addition to *Grandpa Green*, he is the author of *It's a Book*, which has been translated into over 20 languages, *Abe Lincoln's Dream*, *Madam President* and *John, Paul, George & Ben*, among others. He has illustrated a bunch of stuff too: *The True Story of the 3 Little Pigs*, *Math Curse*, Dr. Seuss's *Hooray for Diffendoofer Day!*, *The Very Persistent Gappers of Frip*, *Big Plans*, and *James and the Giant Peach*. He is married to the book designer Molly Leach. [lanesmithbooks.com]

Jon Klassen is an illustrator and author from Ontario, Canada. He has received the Caldecott Medal for his book *This Is Not My Hat* and a Caldecott Honor for his illustrations in *Extra Yarn*, written by Mac Barnett. He also won the Governor General's Award for his illustrations in *Cats' Night Out*, written by Caroline Stutson, and a Geisel Honor for his own book, *I Want My Hat Back*. His other books include *The Dark*, written by Lemony Snicket, and *House Held Up by Trees*, written by Ted Kooser. He lives in Los Angeles. [burstofbeaden.com]

Susan Jeffers, a *New York Times* bestselling artist, has also won numerous awards, including a Caldecott Honor from the American Library Association. Her work has been exhibited in The Metropolitan Museum of Art, the Brooklyn Museum, and the Norman Rockwell Museum. Her books, including *Brother Eagle, Sister Sky*; *The Nutcracker* and Robert Frost's *Stopping by Woods on a Snowy Evening*, have sold millions of copies and have been published around the world. Susan Jeffers (shown far right) lives in Westchester County, New York. [susanjeffers-art.com]

Here is **Steven Kellogg** with one of the English setters in the kennel where he worked when he was a boy. Sixty years later, animals are still an important part of his life and his work. They appear prominently in the more than one hundred books he has published, including *A Rose for Pinkerton*, *Clorinda Takes Flight*, *Farty Marty* and *Is Your Mama a Llama?* Steven Kellogg has been awarded the Regina Medal for his body of work. [stevenkellogg.com]

Erin Stead lives in a hundred-year-old barn in Ann Arbor, Michigan, with her husband, Philip, who is an author and illustrator. Together they created *A Sick Day for Amos McGee*, winner of the 2011 Caldecott Medal, as well as *Bear Has a Story to Tell*. She also illustrated *And Then It's Spring* and *If You Want to See a Whale*, both written by Julie Fogliano. Erin likes to visit the local penguinarium every chance she gets. [erinstead.com]

Lucy Cousins is the multi-award-winning creator of the beloved Maisy series. Her other titles include *Yummy: Eight Favourite Fairy Tales*, a *New York Times Book Review* Best Illustrated Children's Book of the Year, as well as *Hooray for Fish!* and Smarties Book Prize-winner *Jazzy in the Jungle!* Lucy has four children and lives in the countryside in Hampshire with her partner, her beautiful labradoodle Rosie, and three chickens. [maisyfunclub.com]

THE ERIC CARLE MUSEUM OF PICTURE BOOK ART

was founded by Eric and Barbara Carle to inspire a love of art and reading through picture books. In its three galleries, The Carle exhibits original illustrations created by picture book artists from around the world. From the art studio where visitors experiment with their own creative projects to the theatre where picture books come to life on stage, it is clear that this is an art museum that also welcomes children. "It has been said that picture books are an introduction to literature for the very young reader," says Eric Carle. "We also wanted to introduce our youngest guests, so new to museums, to the joys of looking at art." The Carle has a large art collection and picture book and scholarly libraries, as well as educational programmes for families, scholars, educators and children. It is a place to get lost in a book, to discuss a painting and to see a performance. It is a place to share ideas, get creative and feel inspired.

Visit The Eric Carle Museum of Picture Book Art in Amherst, Massachusetts, USA or at carlemuseum.org.

What's Your Favourite Animal?

Now it's your turn!
Have fun creating your own
special animal picture...

You can use
pencils • pens • coloured paper

almost anything –

be as creative as you like!